CAMPFIRE IN A HURRICANE

Shoelace Tying

BRIGHTEST SMILE

Cookie Tossing

10,000 MILE CLUB

Whittling

SURVIVAL

Whistling Dixie

LUNAR SCOUT

LORETTA
★ ★ ★
Ace Pinky Scout

I pledge allegiance
to the pink, from my beret
down to my socks. To tell the truth,
and brush each tooth, and sell
my cookies by the box.

Keith Graves

Scholastic Press • New York

For Dixie, Ace Grandmother
– K.G.

Copyright © 2002 by Keith Graves · All rights reserved.
Published by Scholastic Press, a division of Scholastic Inc.,
Publishers since 1920. SCHOLASTIC, SCHOLASTIC PRESS, and asso-
ciated logos are trademarks and/or registered trademarks of
Scholastic Inc. No part of this publication may be reproduced,
or stored in a retrieval system, or transmitted in any form or by
any means, electronic, mechanical, photocopying, recording,
or otherwise, without written permission of the publisher. For
information regarding permission, write to Scholastic Inc.,
Attention: Permissions Department, 557 Broadway, New York,
NY 10012. · Library of Congress Cataloging-in-Publication Data
· Graves, Keith · Loretta : Ace Pinky Scout / [Keith Graves]. –
1st ed.   p.   cm. · Summary: Loretta, unrelenting perfec-
tionist, is devastated when she fails to earn the Golden
Marshmallow Badge, but her grandmother's picture gives her a
new perspective on things. · ISBN 0-439-36831-6 · [1.
Perfectionism (Personality trait) –Fiction. 2. Self-esteem –
Fiction. 3. Scouts and scouting –Fiction.] I. Title. · PZ7.G77524
Lo 2002 · [E] – dc21   2001049458 · 10 9 8 7 6 5 4 3 2 1 02
03 04 05 06 · Printed in Singapore 46 · First edition, September
2002 · The text type was set in 20-point Badger Bold. Book
design by Kristina "Ace" Albertson

Loretta, ace Pinky Scout
and all-around gung ho gal, was perfect.

Perfection ran in her family.

And Gran had been the most perfect Pinky of all.

Loretta worked hard to be just like Gran.
She kept her uniform clean.

Her tea parties were fab.

She flossed.

She knew her scout manual by heart.

She bench-pressed 375.
(376 if she'd had a big breakfast.)

And she saved the world every Thursday.

You need a **big** time-Out!

Loretta had earned every merit badge
in the known universe . . .

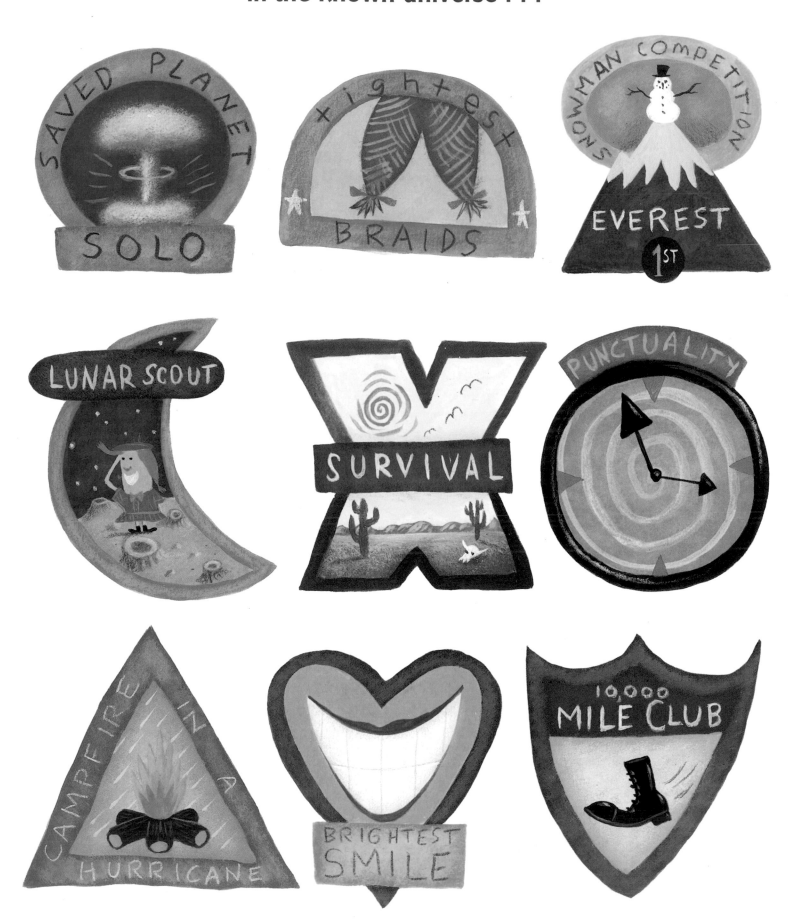

. . . except one. No Pinky sash was complete without the Golden Marshmallow Badge. The only way to get it was at the Annual Tri-county Marshmallow Trials, which happened to be in three days.

Of course, Loretta had been training for months.

She studied.

...so That's it...

She practiced.

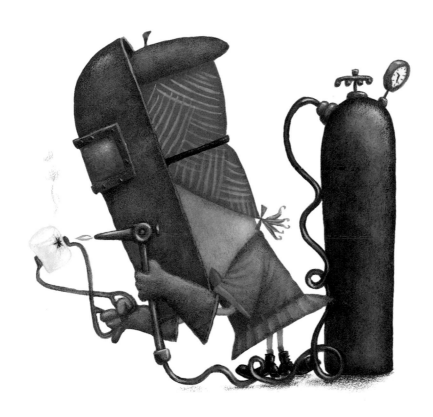

She did one-armed push-ups.

When the big day finally arrived, Loretta was a marshmallow-roasting machine. In seconds her campfire was roaring. She loaded her coat hanger and held it at the perfect aerodynamic angle.

30°

Slowly her marshmallows began to toast.
She could almost feel the new badge on her sash.

Then, the unthinkable happened.

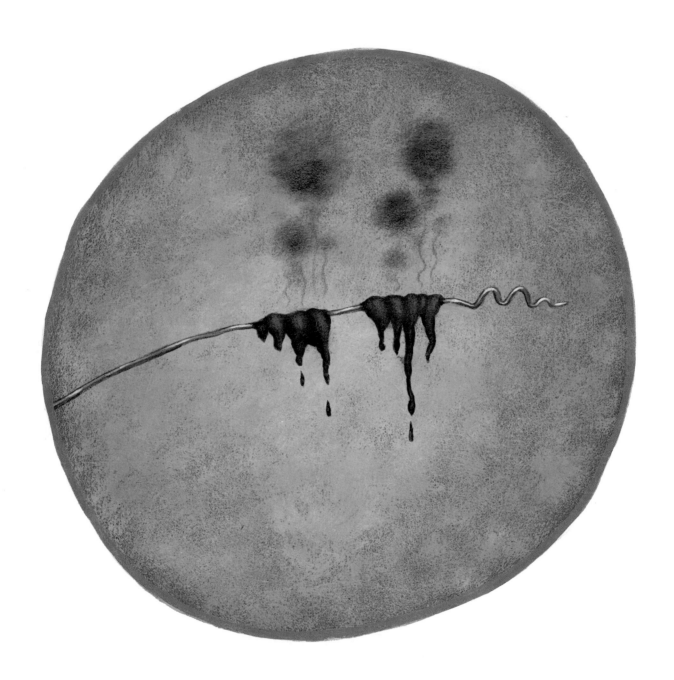

FOOF!

Her marshmallows burst into flames and
turned to smoking black goo.

For the first time ever, Loretta had failed.

She cried for days.

She fell into such a deep funk, she hung up her beret.
"Oh, Gran," she moaned. "I've failed. I'm not a
perfect Pinky like you were. And when it comes to
roasting marshmallows, I really stink."

Then Gran's picture spoke.

"Well, girlfriend, stinking is part of life.
Everyone stinks at something. Even me."

"B-But Gran, I thought you were perfect."
"Nope," said the picture.
"I never could tie a bow. See my tie? It's a clip-on."

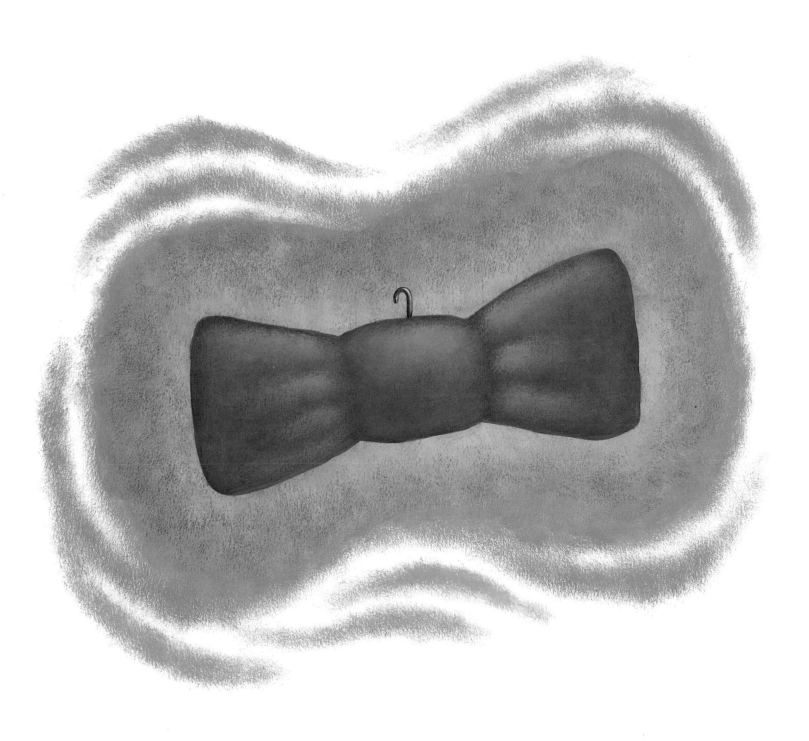

Loretta gasped!

"And your great-aunt
Lenore over there?"
Gran pointed.
"Big hero. But she couldn't
start a campfire
with a blowtorch."

"Your great-great
Granny Lanette
used to save the
world every Tuesday
AND Thursday, too.
But her hair was
a mess."

"And without Cousin Lindsay, George Washington
would never have crossed the Delaware.
But if you look closely at her blouse,
you can see what she had for lunch."

"Looks like lasagna," said Loretta.
"That was her favorite," said Gran.

"Now put that beret back on, kiddo. It's Thursday."
The picture was silent again.
Loretta thought for a minute, and sighed with relief.
Then she blew her nose, pulled up her socks . . .

. . . and ran out to save the world.

Hang on
Human Race,
Loretta's on
the case!

Later, the President awarded Loretta the Congressional *Thanks for Saving the World* Medal.

"Well," thought Loretta, "it's not the Golden Marshmallow, but it does match my barrettes!"

LEXIE

SARGE

PIN

LULU

That night, Loretta looked at
Gran's portrait for a long time.
"Thanks Gran," Loretta whispered,
"for letting me know that all of you stunk, too."
"No sweat, kiddo," the picture whispered back.

That night, Loretta happily went to sleep,
even though she knew she wasn't perfect.

I'm still an ace,
despite my flaw.
Besides, I like my
marshmallows raw.

But there was always tomorrow . . .

Arm Wrestling

Snowman Competition — EVEREST 1st

Musical Composition

tightest BRAIDS

Hand Stand!

SAVED PLANET SOLO

Trauma Treatment

PUNCTUALITY

Sleeping bag Knitting